GREEN BRIER

STORIES THAT RHYME

Written by

Amy Giacchino

Illustrated by

Stella Giacchino

Praise for Greenbrier:
Stories That Rhyme

"We're so grateful to have a daughter as ridiculously
talented and prolific as Amy."
- My Parents, Simultaneously

"None of my checks bounced."
- Stella Giacchino, Illustrator

"If she had spent as much time on this book as she did on
her work, she would've been a great addition to the team."
- Yelena, Former Employer

"Sounds cool."
- Acquaintance, After They Asked Me What I'm Working On

"I really really liked it."
- Alaina, My First Friend

"I've always wanted my life fictionalized through rhyme."
- Zona Heaster Shue, Probably

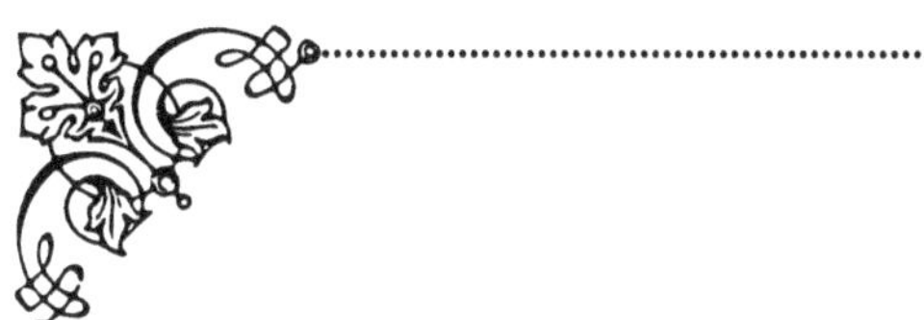

GREENBRIER:
STORIES THAT RHYME

Illustrations by Stella Giacchino

GREENBRIER: STORIES THAT RHYME PAPERBACK EDITION 2025.

for Zona

Part One

The Courting

Part Two

The Conjuring

Part Three

The Convincing

Inspired by the Life

of Zona Heaster Shue

Greenbrier County,
West Virginia

1896

Based on a true story
Of grit and revival,
This tale aims to portray
One ghost's final reprisal.

Bear with me in this,
As I have taken liberties
In order to enhance
The story's festivities.

Be that as it may,
The foundation remains:

A voice beyond the grave
Will set this small town aflame.

One hundred years later,
They still remember her name.

Part One

The Courting

October, 1896

A Bond Brewed

"Is there dirt on my face?"
I thought, wiping my cheek.
His gaze didn't break.
My knees felt weak.

With a grin and a nod,
He walked down the aisle.
"I don't believe we've met,"
He said with a smile.

I blushed in response
To the tall brunette.
My husband and I,
That's how we met.

Smitten with the Smithy

"Mother!"
I called, running through the door,
Shouting in a manner she could not ignore.

"No need to shriek,"
From the kitchen, she replied.

"It's fate we needed coffee—
I'm so in love I could die!"

"Cease the dramatics,
Your life's not a play."

"If only you were there, Mother,
You might be so swayed."

I sighed with affection,
Falling into my chair.

"Dear heavens, child,
Shall I start reciting a prayer?"

"Blue as the sea,
Might I drown in his eyes."

"When have *you* seen the sea?"

"A girl can surmise."

Mother studied my response,
"Whom for this shall I blame?"

"The new blacksmith in town—
Edward Trout Shue is his name.

We must invite him at once,
It's the kind thing to do."

My eyes searched her earnestly,
Hoping she'd approve.

"I'll ask your father before sending a letter.
I'm sure with your persistence,
He'll give in to the pressure."

Sparks Over Supper

Dark waves of hair. A freckle-dotted nose.
One dimpled cheek from a grin tinted rose.

"Do your parents live near, Mr. Shue?" Mother asked.
"Forty miles north with a farm that's quite vast—

And please call me Edward." He looked at me then,
"Having shared a meal, I'd say we're all friends."

"Zona, dear, do you feel well?"
I shook from my daze, released from his spell.

"Yes, Mother," I managed to respond.
"How was your journey?" My dim attempt at a bond.

He sipped from his cup, amused and beguiled,
"Anticipation grew with each stretch of mile."

The remaining hour flew by in an instant,
Our voices entwined in a song so consistent

With that of the birds who sing in the trees,
His lilting words turning into charming melodies.

As the sun set, Mother saw him to the door.
A bow of his head sent me spinning in ardor.

Sense and Spontaneity

"Did I talk enough?" I asked from the floor.
"Does he think me verbose, *or worse*, quite a bore?"

"You're thinking too much—*sit still there*,"
Mother said gently as she brushed through my hair.

"Though he seemed kind, the words he said wise—
I can't help but question that glint in his eye."

"Mother, be calm! You saw it firsthand,
Well-mannered etiquette of a sensible man."

"Sensible is what I expect of his age.
It's his severe affection I find rather strange."

"*Love* is strange! You should be so delighted.
Your daughter admired, her future decided."

"You've known him just *weeks*. After careful assessing,
I can't in good mind give you my blessing."

My heart raced as I spoke, "Mother, I'm twenty-two,
More than mature to assess Mr. Shue.

In rejecting your claim, I don't mean to cause stress,
But if he asked for my hand, *know now I'll say yes*."

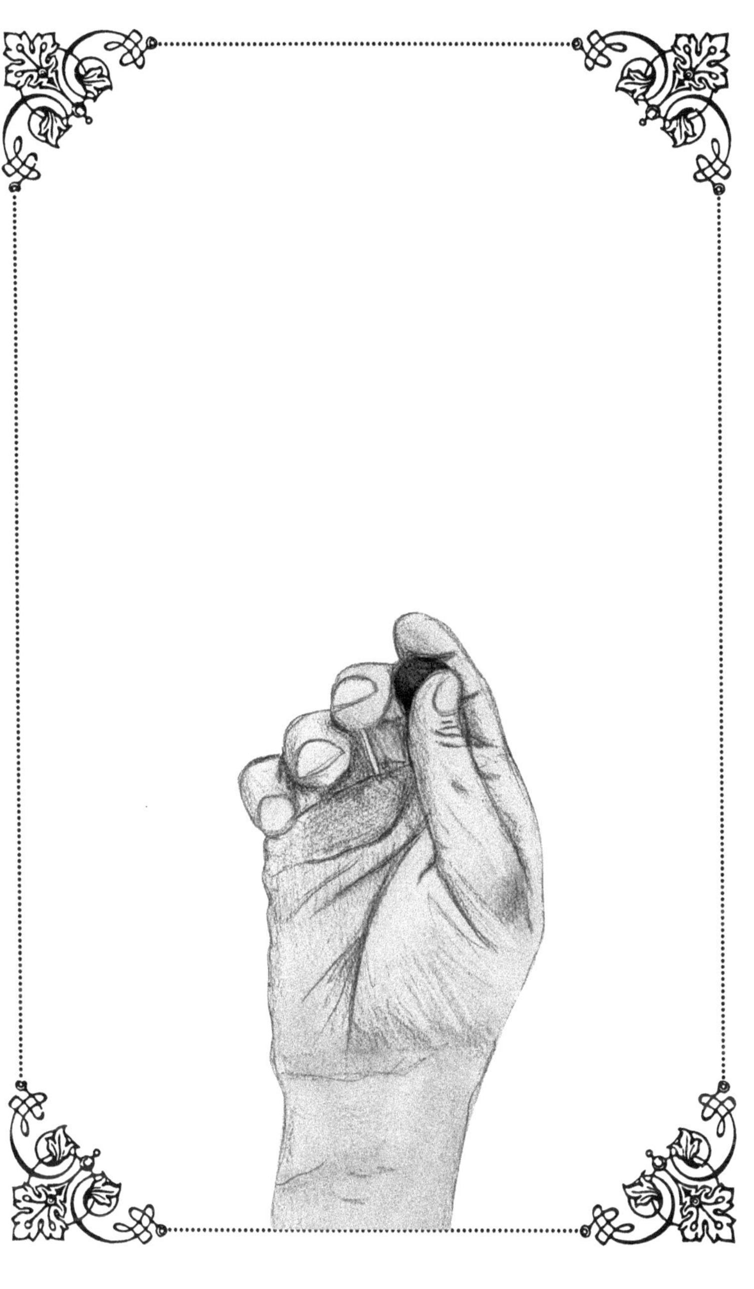

Pebble-Crossed Lovers

Knock.

I turned in my sleep.

Knock.

My eyes fluttered.

Knock.

Bare feet met the floor.

Knock.

Could it be Mother?

Knock.

My body moved slow,

Knock.

As I headed to the window.

Ed beckoned me down,

Arm raised in the air.

With one wave of his hand,

I took to the stairs.

"What are you doing?!"

I whispered excitedly.

Taking my arm,

He explained his pursuit of me:

"While I was in bed,

I couldn't help but conclude,

This afternoon with you

Left me utterly bemused."

My brow furrowed then.

"I believe I'm offended

At this accusation—

That our time together

Induced no precise conversation."

"You misunderstand,
It's not precision I demand."
Pulling me close,
He reached for my hand.

"Your words of sincerity
I found such a rarity.
In just moments together,
You became my true clarity.

I must confess now
My feelings precisely:

You've captured my heart,"
To me he confided,
"I hope you can claim
My love is requited."

With a jump and a shriek,
My lips met his cheek.
Edward and I,
We married that week.

The Crimson Bride

Quiet chattering,
Intimate gathering,
In the town's church
Rose a couple enamoring,

Affirming affections,
Defining connection,
Silence greeted calls
For any objections.

I stood by Ed's side
In a gown of carmine.
'Fore sparsely filled pews,
Our love we described.

"A bond between you
Makes this covenant true."
Declared before God,
We both said, "I do."

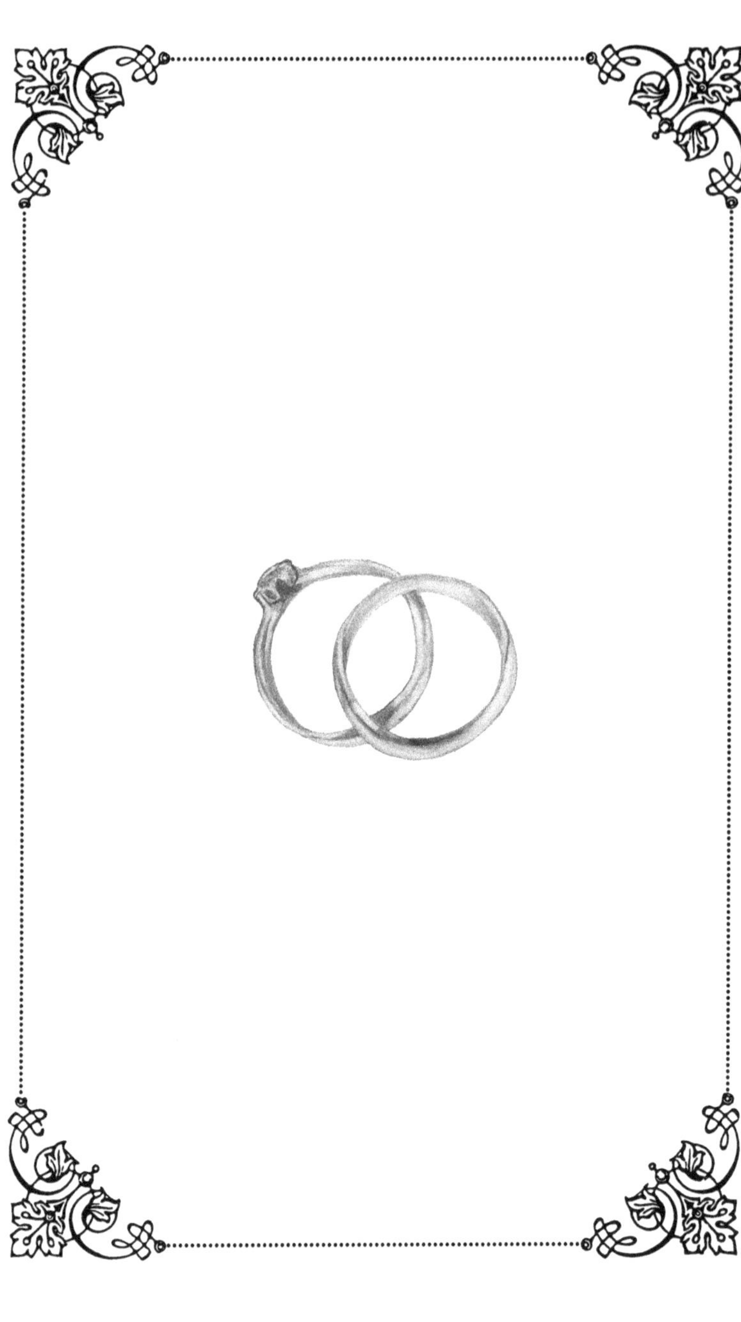

When Love...

The following weeks filled with chores mundane,
Yet while scrubbing the stove, my heart still sang.

Each night from his lips, true love confessed.
In return, I assured the table was set:

Pork roasted just right. Breads graciously buttered.
"How lucky am I," he sighed without stutter.

I sensed Mother's doubt of our true connection.
Though soon, I hoped, he'd change her perception.

His laugh proved infectious. Neighbors he charmed,
Nodding their heads as we passed arm in arm.

It felt almost fictitious, this marriage of mine.

It had just been a month
When I first saw the signs.

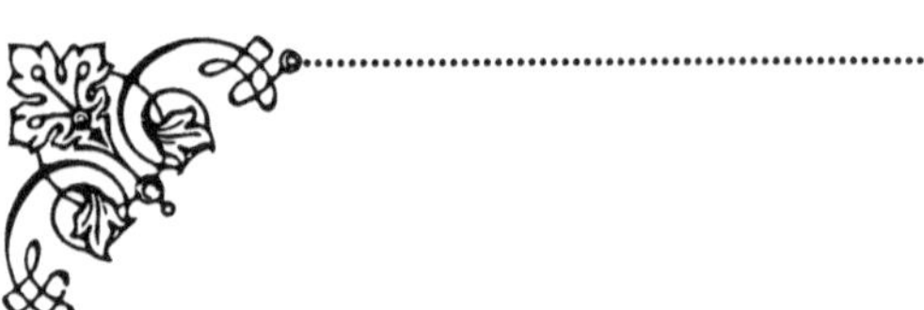

...Turns Sour

Dark-clouded days brought unhappy moods,
Tantrums and protests over distasteful food.

I could not understand the doors that he slammed.
The hands that were raised. The cruel reprimands.

Comments turned harsh. Complaints grew consistent.
"Ungrateful," I was, is what he insisted.

My efforts to amend were oft met with rejection.
His attempts to atone felt void of affection.

It felt years had passed since our window-by greeting.
I questioned my heart—its path misleading.

Just one trait stayed true through his rage and ire:

That glint in his eye
I had once so admired.

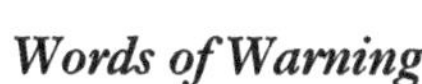

Words of Warning

"He won't allow any visits.
I haven't seen you in ages!
Are you well?" Mother wrote,
Amid tear stains on pages.

"It's not normal, his ways,
The behavior I'm perceiving."

I stopped to consider this
Before I kept reading:

"I'm asking you home,
Your father understands.
Please know in your heart
Things don't always go as planned.

What you have described
Is a marriage unkind,
Deficient in a love
Of which you've been deprived."

I set down the letter.

. . .

What was it I missed
When we first met?
An exchange in an aisle
I'd now come to regret.

Mother's doubts proved true.
How I ignored her mentions,
His ingratiating nature—
A cunning invention.

"Write me back soon,"
Her strokes intertwined,
"I'll be looking for your letter."
Was Mother's closing line.

Folding her words,
I thought of home.
Bathed in the memory
As steps sounded below.

The Fight

I learned to hate my name,
Each successive exchange.
His lips turning vowels
Once familiar, now strange.

Tonight was no different.
He came home belligerent,
Slurring his words
With verbs inconsiderate.

This behavior I knew
Not to be misconstrued.
I braced myself then
For the rage to ensue.

He stumbled inside
With an uncertain stride.
A fist on the table
Began the night's chide:

"Is this my reward
After the *hours* I've spent?
An indolent wife
With a talent to torment!"

He took a step closer,
"You prepared only bread?"
Gesturing madly,
Ale on his breath.

"I've had enough
Of this idle trend!"
I turned from his rage,
Praying for its end.

He shifted so slightly,
The raise of an arm.
It took only a moment
Before I saw the stars.

The Boy Next Door

Ed spoke in haste.
To the neighbor nearby,
Between hurried breaths,
The task he defined:

"I'm here for a favor
'Fore I head to the store.
Could you call on my wife
With a knock on our door?"

The boy nodded and said,
"I can leave in a few,
Once my mother returns,
If it's no difference to you."

"I'd prefer you go soon,
For I need to get back—
Noting what she needs
Is all that I ask."

"Then I'll see to her now,"
And off the boy flew,
Running up the hill
To find Mrs. Shue.

. . .

A hand tugged his shirt.
"What is it now?"
In reply the boy froze,
Then mumbled aloud:

"I need to tell you,
I just saw Mrs. Shue.
She looked kind of funny,
Her skin kind of blue."

Ed questioned his account.
The boy whispered, still stunned,

*"Under her head,
I swear I saw blood."*

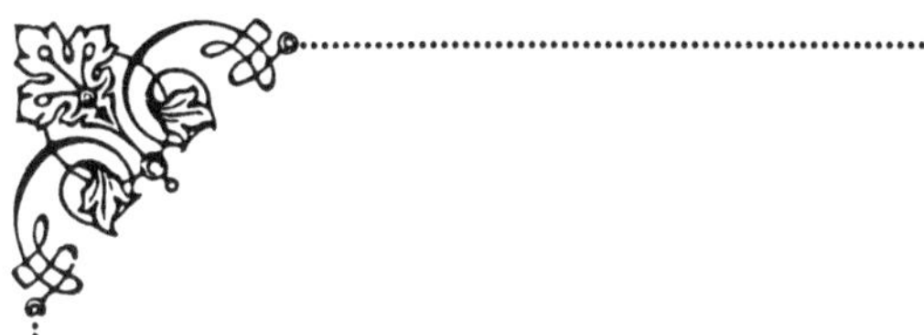

Part Two

The Conjuring

January, 1897

Beyond the Grave

I was lying on the floor,
That much I could see.
The familiar sight
Of my ceiling greeted me.

As I detached my back
From weathered wood,
Thoughts filled my head,
Memories of childhood.

Something felt different.
I'd been betrayed.
I turned my head
And met my own gaze.

This version of me,

She looked cold and distant.

Grief swelled my stomach—

A testament to my nonexistence.

Tear stains on blanched cheeks,

Limbs stiff and angled,

Torn wool stockings,

Dark hair in tangles.

My pallid neck

Was blushed with red.

"Yes," I thought,

"I am definitely dead."

A Convincing Show

Ed burst through the door,
Bellowing my name,
"Zona, Zona!"
As if playing a game.

My body lay still,
An arm across my chest.
He hovered over me,
Tears soaking my dress.

It did look convincing,
This *performance* he was attempting:
A devoted husband,
Ardent and unsuspecting.

I almost believed it—
Shaking the thought aside,
Remembering quickly
He was the reason I died.

Mother Gets a Letter

She assumed the worst
When the letter arrived,
Informing her gently
Her daughter had died.

A knife in her gut,
She fell to the ground.
Out from her chest
Came a ghastly sound.

Paused on a phrase,
Cause of death explained:

"Childbirth," it read,
Underlined on the page.

How could she not know?
Grief-ravaged, distraught.
Her daughter with child.
She ached at the thought.

Suspicions at a Funeral

Not once did Ed leave,
A widower grieved,
Guarding my body,
His hand on my cheek.

Sympathies muttered
For tragedy suffered.
"They were married just months,"
Neighbors quietly uttered.

Mother studied the room,
My crimson costume—
The same dress that I wore
When I first said, "I do."

What she didn't expect,
An addition suspect,
One scarf neatly tied
In a bow round my neck.

The pastor was brief,
Relaying their grief,
Promising one day
Again we will meet.

Few stayed behind
As my body declined
Back into the earth.
Mother started to cry.

It was then he slipped out.
Without making a sound,
Without saying farewell,
Ed took off into town.

A sense of deceit,
My death incomplete.
Next to my grave,
Mother laid down a wreath.

Sending a Sign

Back at her house,

I watched Mother work,
Wringing out sheets,
The ones that had lain
Beneath my cold feet.

Soaking with soap,
She scrubbed at the threads,
When it suddenly seemed
The sheets became red.

Mother shrieked at the sight!
While water splashed clear,
Cotton turned crimson—
My attempt to interfere.

She stood there in shock
At a message ill-defined.
I thought to myself,
"She might need another sign."

Visiting Hours

Later that night,

Mother was restless,
Drifting out of sleep.
Consciousness weaving,
Tossing between sheets,

When a hushed invocation
Slipped under her door,
Taking the form
Of a glistening orb.

"Mother," I whispered,
Having stirred her awake.
My orb then dispersed,
Forming a familiar shape.

Rubbing her eyes,
Mother gasped at the sight:
Her beloved daughter
Cast in brilliant light.

"*Mother,*" I echoed,
Robed in the same red
As the day I had died.
Mother sprang from the bed.

My skin felt alive.
My dress textured lace.
Mother started to cry
At the sight of my face.

"Tell me, daughter,
What truly happened?"
A pause between us.
"Is it worse than I imagined?"

I felt my throat close,
"You were right all along."
With a shudder and sigh,
My light was gone.

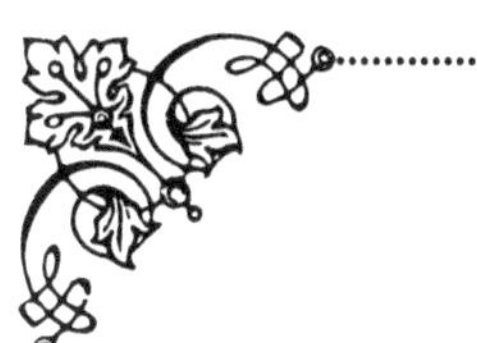

. . .

The following night,
Mother stared at the door,
Awaiting a sign,
A light from the floor.

Granting her prayer,
From a luminous sphere,
Beaming into the room,
Once again I appeared.

"Please, I must know,"
With tears, Mother begged.
Fearing disbelief,
I chose trust instead.

Closing my eyes,
Truth on my side,
I began to describe
The night I had died:

"It was half past five
When Edward arrived.
I was setting the table,
Not unlike every night.

Already incensed,
He took great offense
To the meal I had made.
Thus, outrage commenced.

Plates crashed on floors,
Knives thrown at doors.
From inadequate aliment,
Bred a raucous storm.

Before I could speak,
His hand met my cheek.
The world went dark,
A practiced technique.

Thinking I'd drowned,
I woke on the ground.
Fingers crushed bone
With a deafening sound.

No breath could I form.
No one could I warn.
Hands gripped me hard
As I started to mourn.

He caused this atrocity,
Affirmed my mortality,"
I displayed my truth then
To refute any fallacy.

Mother stood stunned
By this grim observation:

*My neck turned around
In one complete rotation.*

. . .

I returned twice more,
The shock minimized,
Retelling my story
With details memorized.

Mother listened, attuned,
Engrossed and consumed,
Absorbing the words
Of a woman entombed.

By the fourth night,
I shared my intention,
A crucial exclamation
To define my position:

"Call widespread attention,
Alert the physician—
They have it all wrong.
Let this be my proposition."

Mother's Mission

My frequent apparition
Raised wide superstition.
Whispered across roads,
A corpse's admission:

"One dinner displeasing
Caused anger unceasing.
He held onto her neck
Until she stopped breathing!"

Lips brushing ears
Led to ubiquitous fear.
From neighbors' eyes
Fell sympathetic tears.

That's when she set out
To raise considerable doubt.
For the local attorney,
Mother recited her account:

"Sir, she came to me, you see,

It's hard to believe, I agree,

But I know my own daughter.

I'm the one who lost her.

Her heart was gold,

But his hands were stronger."

. . .

"Mrs. Heaster,

I'm not one to be gullible,

But your loss is incalculable.

The neighbors are knocking

For a cause more explicable.

I hear what you're saying,

The cause of death you're conveying.

Let's call on the doctor,

Perhaps he can do some explaining."

Doctor's Orders

"It's true, Mr. Shue,
Did not only refuse,
But completely forbade
A thorough review.

Before I arrived,
He thought it sound
To dress her to the neck
In a burgundy gown.

He was rather abrupt,
Having so rushed
Her body upstairs
Before I could construct

A plausible cause
For her untimely death.
I did what I could
To bring back her breath.

'No more examinations,

No further observations!'

He yelled to the room,

A grieving declaration.

Out of respect,

I thought it best to resist

The feeling there's something

I might have dismissed.

Mrs. Shue *had* inquired

About a condition desired.

I wrote what I assumed

In past nights transpired.

But if her Mother insists,

I do feel compelled

To exhume her body

And see for ourselves."

The Autopsy

It's a unique experience:

The atmosphere serious.
Men chattering over marks mysterious.

I watched them pick as they pruned and stripped.
Each flick of their tools made my body wince.

Ed loomed in the corner, eyes fixed on his hands.
He looked up not once throughout the exam.

Past shoulders I stared, my heart already prepared.
"She wasn't with child," one man declared.

"That's not all," the doctor disclosed,

"There's bone broken here."
My neck now exposed.

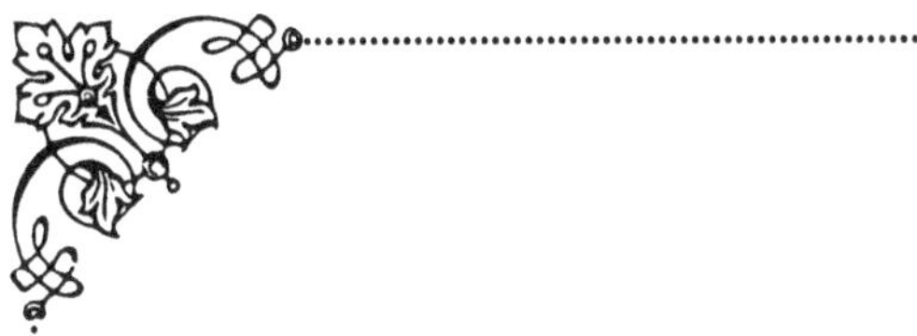

Part Three

The Convincing

June, 1897

A Circumstantial Situation

The trees had changed since the arrest was made,
Magnolias bloomed as anticipation plagued.

Ed smirked with conceit as jurors took seats.
Attorneys' statements stifled tapping feet.

Presented with facts, the presumed violent act,
Edward proudly denied with shoulders relaxed.

He laughed at the claim. "Anyone could be blamed
With such fragile evidence!" the defendant exclaimed.

The votes were received, stating most jurors agreed.
An indictment commenced. "Not guilty," was his plea.

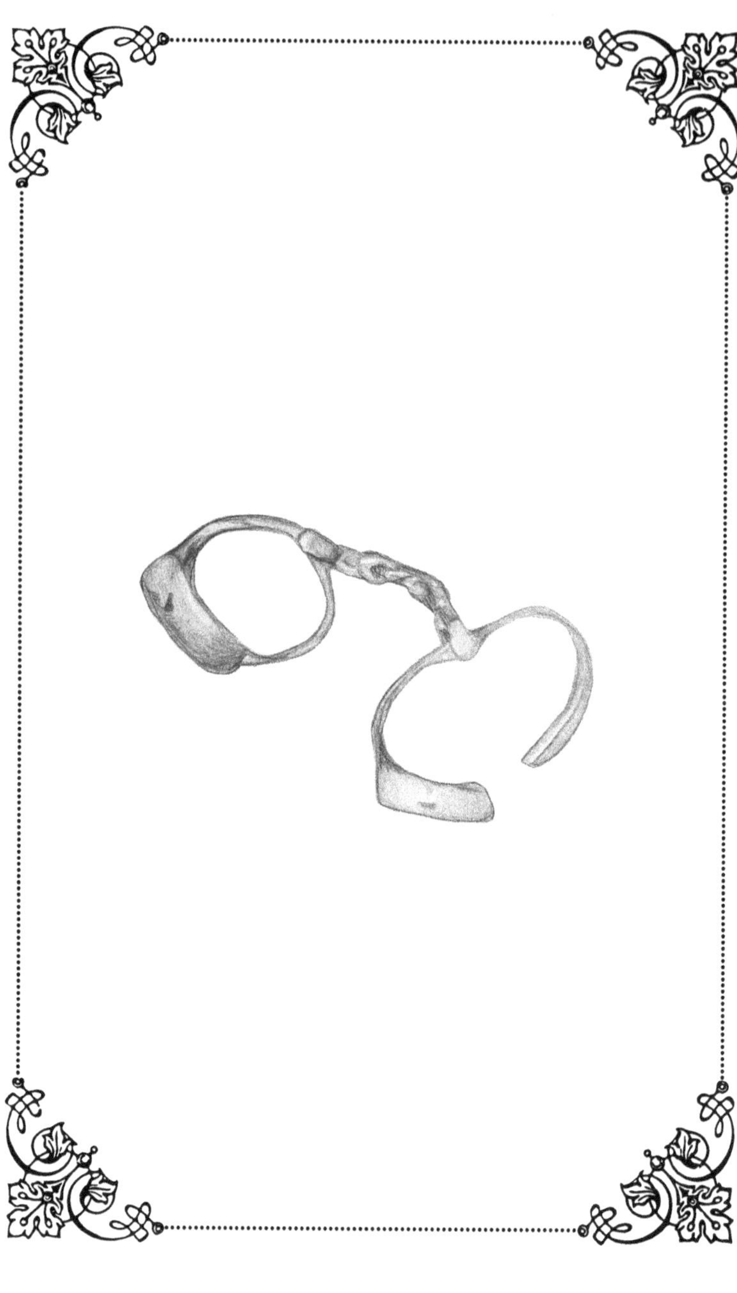

Pre-Trial Wiles

From the depths of his cell, Ed managed to tell
Whispers of contempt in an attempt to dispel:

"This theory's absurd! The boy found her first.
I was not even home when the incident occurred!

Our life interrupted by a person corrupted,
Destructive and cruel. A neighbor mistrusted.

We all know the type—men broadly disliked,
Preying on women to counter life's gripes.

I could count more than one hundred friends
Who would speak kindly in my defense.

This ghoulish nonsense only a fool could invent.
Wrongly punishing me is its sole intent."

His words weaved their way through a town of dismay.
From the foot of her bed, I watched Mother pray.

Some said she's insane, having endured all that pain.
A woman bereaved, her grief unrestrained.

Others, amused, having tales to enthuse,
Gabbing profusely over provocative news.

I watched them pick sides:

An isolated bride,
Whose mother couldn't cope
With the fact she had died.

Or should they listen
To the strange apparition
Who came back to proclaim
One harrowing admission.

Day One:

Specter Versus Shue

Twelve men selected

Reviewed evidence collected.

Crowds congregated

To observe the suspected.

One man accused

Stepped in the courtroom.

Witnesses were called.

Two testified by noon.

The motive explicable.

The action condemnable.

His lawyer long argued

For evidence inadmissible.

At the end of the day,

They called out her name.

Mother rose from the pew,

With courage untamed.

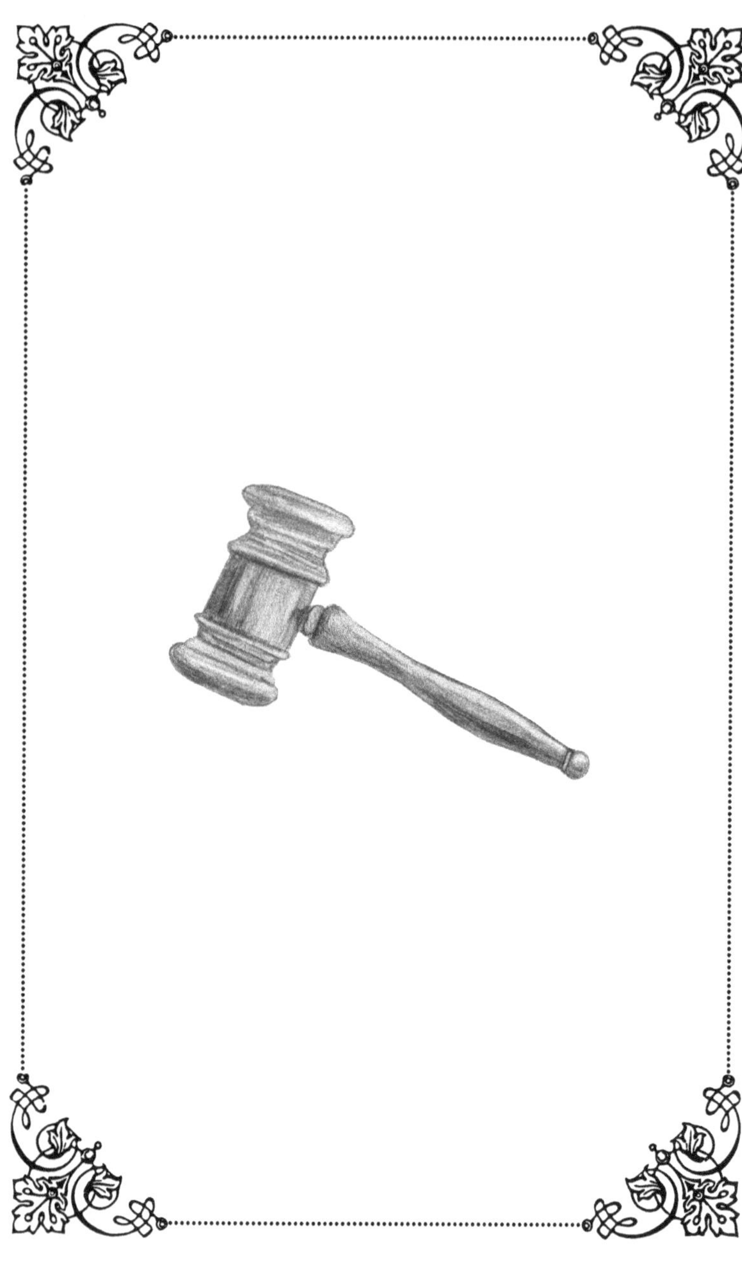

Defense Attorney:

"Is it true what they say,

You dreamed of her *ghost?*

To neighbors and strangers,

A most riveting boast!

Your daughter returned

With stories to tell,

Defining her death

Until you knew it well

Enough to convince

The soundest of minds.

I must say I admire

The details you've designed.

Jurors, I ask

For your honesty.

Do you really believe

In this *phantom progeny?*"

Mother:

"Sir, if I may,
You did ask me first,
If it's true, my encounter,
In which you seem ill-versed.

It was no dream,
Despite what you've heard,
Only genuine details
I assure you occurred.

Not one night, but four,
She appeared at my door,
Revealing a crime
I could not ignore."

She turned to the jury,
"Would you do the same,
If it were your child
Who met mine own's fate?"

Ghosts of Husband's Past

Rumors had spread
Since the start of the trial.
"This was his *third* wife!"
No lips in town idle.

Friends of Ed mentioned,
With little discretion,
He said he was destined
Not one wife, but seven.

Chittering sounds
Of a previous life.
Long before me,
Edward caused women strife:

First, there was Allie,
A kind, reserved lady.
They'd been married a year
When she had their first baby.

Ed's moods grew unstable,
Distressing his spouse.
By eighteen eighty-eight,
He kicked her out of the house.

Later that year,
Allie filed for divorce
While Ed was in jail
For stealing a horse.

Next there was Lucy,
Who was not yet sixteen.
Ed hoped that her age
Compelled naivety.

"I was mending the roof,"
Is what Ed had said,
"When a brick slipped off
And fell on her head."

Her family suspected
His grief-stricken front,
As they buried young Lucy,
His wife of eight months.

They said I was third,
Whose love could not sate
Ed's ravenous greed
Is what sealed my fate.

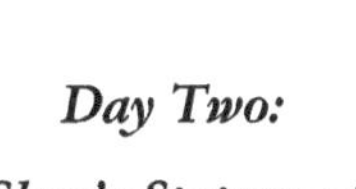

Day Two:

Shue's Statement

Ed took the stand at a quarter past two.
His melodious voice played a familiar tune:

"You must understand," to the jury he said,
"*I loved my wife*—you've all been misled.

I stand by my vows from the day we wed.
Excuse me," he sniffled, bowing his head.

"Every night without her feels like it's the end.
I dread coming home to our empty bed.

Can you imagine the pain I've suffered since?
Not saying goodbye or sharing a last kiss.

If she did return, her beloved spirit,
It would be *me* whom she'd choose to visit."

. . .

God, he's persuasive. I examined their faces,
Studying eyes for suspicious traces.

The jury stood up after Ed left the stand,
Shuffling away into a room on command.

I counted the seconds until they returned.
An hour and ten minutes. My ears started to burn.

One man met the judge to submit their decision.
Voices fell silent. Bodies stiffened.

I watched Mother gasp as the man faced the pews.
"We find the defendant guilty."

It was the first time I saw him lose.

Casket Closed

Condolences awaited,
Collective doubt sated,
Leaving Mother to mourn
The death he created.

Was this the end?
After weeks she had spent
Combating his lies
In her daughter's defense.

"It's over," she said,
A hand to her chest.
Mother looked at the sky,
"It's your time to rest."

I smiled at her,
An indebted response,
Eternally grateful
For the chance to move on.

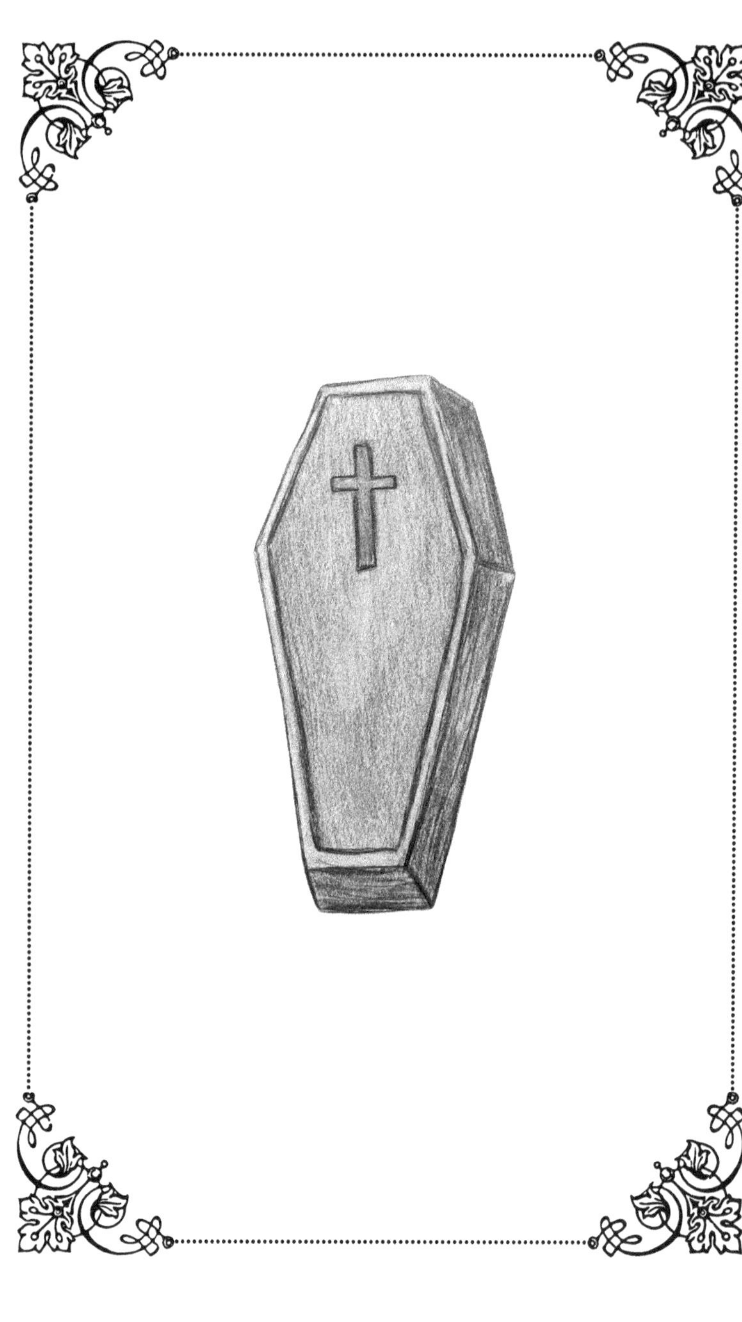

Epilogue

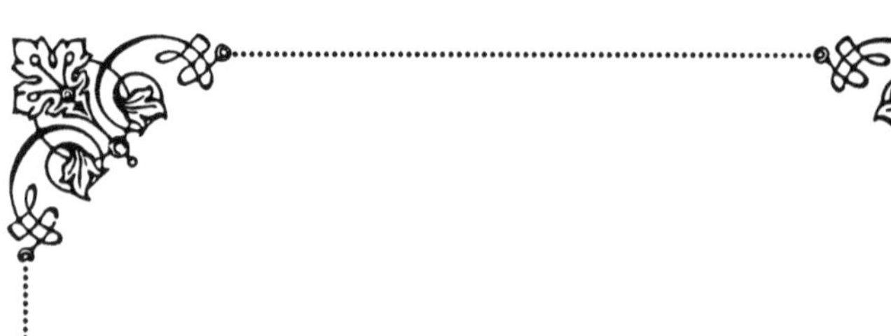

March, 1900

A Man Unremarkable

Alone in his cell
Is where Ed met his end.
An unknown epidemic
Ensured last days ill-spent.

Three years had passed
Since the ghost of his wife
Sent him to prison
For the rest of his life.

No family appeared
To claim his remains.
Therefore, he was buried
Beneath an unmarked grave.

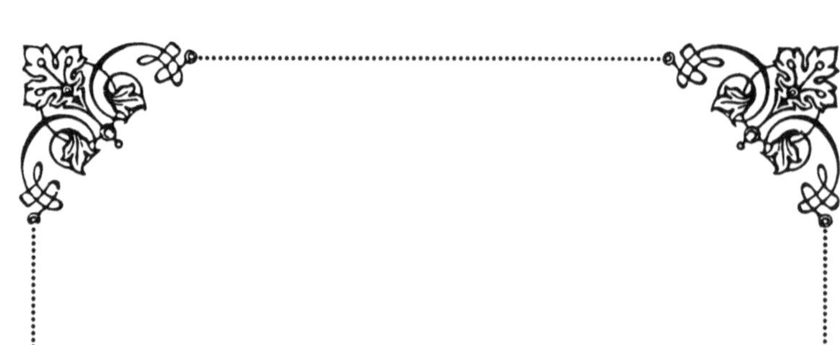

The End

Skeptics have mentioned,
Countered and questioned
The truth of this tale—
One mother's invention?

They thought it composed
In effort to expose
The man she believed
Was at fault for her woes.

Others objected,
Having accepted
Her daughter returned,
Four times resurrected.

Nevertheless,
It is the one time,
On record defined,
A ghost did convince
Twelve men of a crime.

What you have read
Is a story inspired
By a real human being
Turned ghost I admire.

It's hard to condense
A woman's lifetime
In just sixty pages,
Through only rhyme.

Thus, there are details
That have gone unsaid,
Like particular mentions
Of Zona's life before Ed.

If you'd like to learn more,
What others have to say,
Read through the sources
Listed on the next page.

Sources and Related Texts

The Haunting of Zona Heaster Shue:
The Greenbrier Ghost Chronicles
by Nancy Richmond and Misty Murray-Walkup

The Greenbrier Ghost: And Other Strange Stories
by Dennis Deitz

Greenbrier Ghost, Zona Heaster Shue
Greenbrier Valley West Virginia
by Belinda Anderson

The Greenbrier Ghost Reexamined
Greenbrier Historical Society
by Arabeth Balasko

Lore Podcast
Episode 39: Take the Stand
by Aaron Mahnke

Unexplained Mysteries Podcast
The Greenbrier Ghost Pt. 1 & Pt. 2
by Molly Brandenburg & Richard Rossner

The Unquiet Grave
by Sharyn McCrumb

Historical Mentions

The following points I'd like to emphasize,
Facts of the story important to recognize:

Edward's full name was Erasmus Stribbling Trout Shue.
According to sources, he preferred to go by "Edward" or "Trout."

Zona's full name was Elva Zona Heaster Shue. She went by "Zona."

Zona's death was initially recorded as an "everlasting faint" before the
local doctor, George Knapp, officially changed it to "childbirth."

James P.D. Gardner, one of the lawyers who defended Edward in his
trial, was the first Black attorney to practice law in a Greenbrier court.
Author Sharyn McCrumb wrote a historical fiction novel, The Unquiet
Grave, inspired by his life.

Edward was not Zona's first love. Sources say she was pregnant by a
man named George Wooldridge over a year before meeting Edward.
There is no further record of the child.

Many years have passed since this ghostly occasion,
Resulting in quite a few varying interpretations.

I hope my version serves Zona well,
If not, I'll assume she'll come tell me herself.

Soule Chapel United Methodist Church in
Greenbrier County, West Virginia

Zona Heaster Shue's tombstone at
Soule Chapel Cemetery

Soule Chapel Cemetery in Greenbrier County, West Virginia

Articles and photos from Soule Chapel depicting the
church's history and associations with Zona Heaster Shue

Thank you David and Pat for your stories and hospitality

The Greenbrier Ghost historical marker off of
Route 60 near Smoot, West Virignia

Historical marker for the Greenbrier County
Courthouse where Shue's trial took place in 1897

Foul Play Suspected.

Mrs. Zona (Heaster) Shue died in the Richlands of this county, on the 23rd of January, and her body was taken out to Little Sewell and buried. Since then rumors in the community caused the authorities to suspect that she may not have died from natural causes. In short her husband, E. S., commonly known as "Trout" Shue, was suspected of having brought about her death by violence or in some way unknown to her friends. An inquest was accordingly ordered, and, on Monday last before Justice Homer McClung and a jury of inquest, assisted by Mr. Preston, the State's Attorney for the county, Mrs. Shue's body was exhumed and a *post mortem* examination made, conducted by Drs. Knapp, Rupert and Houston McClung, Shue being present and summoned as a witness. From one of the Doctors we learn that the examination clearly disclosed the fact that Mrs. Shue's neck had been broken. We hear too that Shue's conduct at the time of his wife's death and when she lay a corpse in his house was very suspicious.

The jury found in accordance with the facts above stated, charged Shue with the crime of murder and yesterday afternoon he was brought here by James C. Shawver, John N. McClung and Estill McClung and lodged in jail to await the action of the grand jury.

Greenbrier Independent

Published Thursday, June 17, 1897

Shue's Trial Announcement

The trial of "Trout" Shue, for the murder of his wife, is set for Wednesday next, the second day of our Court. It is said that Shue has had 120 witnesses summoned.

Articles found on Newspapers.com

Mrs. Mary J. Heaster, the Mother of Mrs. Shue, Sees her Daughter in Visions.

The following very remarkable testimony was given by Mrs Heaster on the pending trial of E. S. Shue for the murder of his wife, her daughter, and led to the inquest and post mortem examination, which resulted in Shue's arrest and trial. It was brought out by counsel for the accused :

Question.—I have heard that you had some dream or vision which led to this post mortem examination?

Answer.—They saw enough theirselves without me telling them. It was no dream—she came back and told me that he was mad that she didn't have no meat cooked for supper. But she said she had plenty, and said that she had butter and apple-butter, apples and named over two or three kinds of jellies, pears and cherries and raspberry jelly, and she says I had plenty ; and she says don't you think that he was mad and just took down all my nice things and packed them away and just ruined them. And she told me where I could look down back of Aunt Martha Jones', in the meadow, in a rocky place ; that I could look in a cellar behind some loose plank and see. It was a square log house, and it was hewed up to the square, and she said for me to look right at the right-hand side of the door as you go in and at the right-hand corner as you go in. Well, I saw the place just exactly as she told me, and I saw blood right there where she told me ; and she told me something about that meat every night she came, just as she did the first night. She cames four times, and four nights ; but the second night she told me that her neck was squeezed off at the first joint and it was just as she told me.

Q.—Now, Mrs. Heaster, this sad affair was very particularly impressed upon your mind, and there was not a moment during your waking hours that you did not dwell upon it ?

A.—No, sir ; and there is not yet, either.

Q.—And was this not a dream founded upon your distressed condition of mind ?

A.—No, sir. It was no dream, for I was as wide awake as I ever was.

Q.—Then if not a dream or dreams, what do you call it ?

A.—I prayed to the Lord that she might come back and tell me what had happened ; and I prayed that she might come herself and tell on him.

Q.—Do you think that you actually saw her in flesh and blood ?

A.—Yes, sir, I do. I told them the very dress that she was killed in, and when she went to leave me she turned her head completely around and looked at me like she wanted me to know all about it. And the very next time she came back to me she told me all about it. The first time she came, she seemed that she did not want to tell me as much about it as she did afterwards. The last night she was there she told me that she did everything she could do, and I am satisfied that she did do all that, too.

Q.—Now, Mrs. Heaster, don't you know that these visions, as you term them or describe them, were nothing more or less than four dreams founded upon your distress ?

A.—No, I don't know it. The Lord sent her to me to tell it. I was the only friend that she knew she could tell and put any confidence it ; I was the nearest one to her. He gave me a ring that he pretended she wanted me to have ; but I don't know what dead woman he might have taken it off of. I wanted her own ring and he would not let me have it.

Q.—Mrs. Heaster, are you positively sure that these are not four dreams?

A.—Yes, sir. It was not a dream. I don't dream when I am wide awake, to be sure; and I know I saw her right there with me.

Q.—Are you not considerably superstitious?

A.—No, sir, I'm not. I was never that way before, and am not now.

Q.—Do you believe the scriptures?

A.—Yes, sir. I have no reason not to believe it.

Q.—And do you believe the scriptures contain the words of God and his Son?

A.—Yes, sir, I do. Don't you believe it?

Q.—Now, I would like if I could, to get you to say that these were four dreams and not four visions or appearances of your daughter in flesh and blood?

A.—I am not going to say that; for I am not going to lie.

Q.—Then you insist that she actually appeared in flesh and blood to you upon four different occasions?

A.—Yes, sir.

Q.—Did she not have any other conversation with you other than upon the matter of her death?

A.—Yes, sir, some other little things. Some things I have forgotten—just a few words. I just wanted the particulars about her death, and I got them.

Q.—When she came did you touch her?

A.—Yes, sir. I got up on my elbows and reached out a little further, as I wanted to see if people came in their coffins, and I sat up and leaned on my elbow and there was light in the house. It was not a lamp light. I wanted to see if there was a coffin, but there was not. She was just like she was when she left this world. It was just after I went to bed, and I wanted her to come and talk to me, and she did. This was before the inquest and I told my neighbors. They said she was exactly as I told them she was.

Q.—Had you ever seen the premises where your daughter lived?

A.—No, sir, I had not; but I found them just exactly as she told me it was, and I never laid eyes on that house until since her death. She told me this before I knew anything of the buildings at all.

Q.—How long was it after this when you had these interviews with your daughter until you did see buildings?

A.—It was a month or more after the examination. It has been a little over a month since I saw her.

RE-CROSS EXAMINATION.

Q.—You said your daughter told you that down by the fence in a rocky place you would find some things?

A.—She said for me to look there. She didn't say I would find some things, but for me to look there.

Q.—Did she tell you what to look for?

A.—No, she did not. I was so glad so see her I forgot to ask her.

Q.—Have you ever examined that place since?

A.—Yes, sir. We looked at the fence a little but didn't find anything.

Shue Convicted of Murder.

After an elaborate argument of the evidence by Messrs. Gilmer and Preston for the State and Jas. P. D. Gardner, colored, and Dr. Rucker for the accused, the case of the State vs. E. S. (" Trout") Shue was given to the jury last Thursday afternoon, and the jury, after being out one hour and ten minutes, returned into Court with a verdict of murder in the first degree, as charged in the indictment, but recommending that the accused be punished by imprisonment, which means, under the law, that he be confined in the penitentiary for the term of his natural life. Dr. Rucker entered a motion for a new trial, but this was withdrawn the next morning, and Shue will be duly sentenced before the Court adjourns.—Though the evidence was entirely circumstantial, the verdict meets general approval, as all who heard the evidence are satisfied of the prisoner's guilt.—After the murder Shue had every opportunity to make his escape, as four weeks elapsed before he was arrested and put in jail. The fact that he did not do so was explained by Mr. Gilmer, in his argument, by showing that Shue was all the time laboring under the impression that he could not be convicted on circumstantial evidence, and felt secure in knowing that there was no witness but himself, to the crime. This Mr. Gilmer argued, showed not a lack of sense, but information, and accounts for Shue's presence at the inquest and his oft repeated remark that they could not show he did it.

Taking the verdict of the jury as ascertaining the truth, then we must conclude that Shue deliberately broke his wife's neck—probably with his strong hands—and with no other motive than to be rid of her that he might get another more to his liking. And, if so, his crime is one of the most horrible, cruel and revolting ever known in the history of this county.

Mr. Preston deserves the thanks of the people for his diligence in hunting up the evidence and for his admirable management of the case before the jury.

Article found on Newspapers.com

Strange Case of Conviction.

Rancevorte, W. Va., July 3.—Some time ago the wife of E. S. Shue was found dead in her home here. A coroners jury rendered a verdict, "death by heart disease." Neighbors were not satisfied, the woman's body was exhumed and her neck was found broken. Shue was arrested and convicted and sentenced to the penitentiary for life. The principal direct evidence was that of Shue's mother-in-law, who testified that her daughter's spirit had come to her at a seance and said Shue had killed her by breaking her neck. All the other evidence was purely circumstantial.

The Fort Worth Record and Register in Texas
Published Sunday, July 4, 1897

Jailed by Spirit Evidence.

E. S. Shue has been sent to prison from Rancevert, W. Va., by the evidence of a "spirit." His wife was found dead and a jury declared she died of "death by heart disease." Neighbors were not satisfied, so the woman's body was exhumed and the neck was found broken. Shue was arrested and was convicted and sentenced to the penitentiary for life. The principal direct evidence was that of Shue's mother-in-law, who testified that her daughter's spirit had come to her at a seance and said Shue had killed her by breaking her neck.

Moorhead Daily News in Minnestota
Published Tuesday, August 24, 1897

Thank You

To all my lovely friends and family, who read and re-read this book so I could publish it within a reasonable deadline.

To my cousin, Stella Giacchino, for aiding me with her artistic skills so we could bring this book to life.

To the residents of Greenbrier County, for your kindness and generosity throughout our stay.

To the writers and researchers of Zona's story, who helped me entwine historical details with rhyming stanzas.

And finally,
To Zona—without her,
I would have no story to tell.

For more Stories That Rhyme, visit:
www.storiesthatrhyme.com